Postman Pat

to the Rescue

Story by **John Cunliffe**
Pictures by **Celia Berridge**

from the original Television designs by **Ivor Wood**

ANDRE DEUTSCH

First published 1986 by
André Deutsch Limited
105-106 Great Russell Street London WC1B 3LJ
Third impression 1987

Phototypeset by Tradespools Limited, Frome, Somerset
Printed in Great Britain by Cambus Litho, East Kilbride, Scotland

British Library Cataloguing in Publication Data

Cunliffe, John
    Postman Pat to the rescue.
    I. Title   II. Berridge, Celia
    823'.914 [J]   PZ7

ISBN 0 233 97767 8

The day had started cloudy in Greendale, but as Pat set out along the valley, on the way to the village post-office, the sun began to come out. Pat's red van went twisting and turning along the windy roads. He went through Greendale Forest, where all the birds were singing. He went round the sharp corner by Garner Hall, then put his brakes on, hard.

There was a big van almost blocking the road. It was Sam's mobile shop.

"It's going to be a tight squeeze," said Pat. He drove on to the grass at the edge of the road. Sam popped his head round the corner of his van. He waved Pat on.

"Come on!" he shouted. "You've got plenty of room!" Pat wasn't so sure. He edged slowly alongside Sam's van.

"Left a bit!" called Sam. "A bit more. Left . . . left . . . right . . . straighten up . . . keep going, you're OK. Come on, come on . . . that's it."

Pat stopped by Sam's van, and opened his window.

"Hello, Sam," he said. "Thanks for seeing me through. Could you give Mrs. Atkinson her letters please?"

"Right-o, Pat. Mind how you go. Cheerio!"

Sam went off with Mrs. Atkinson's letters and groceries. Pat tried to drive away, but the van didn't move.

"Oh dear," said Pat, putting his head out of the window. He could see the wheel whizzing round and sinking down into the muddy ground. "I think we're stuck."

He revved the engine again, but the wheel just went deeper in.

"Now we are stuck. It's all that rain. It's made the ground boggy."

Sam came back.

"Hello, Pat! Still here?"

"Yes, I am," said Pat, "I'm stuck."

"Don't worry," said Sam. "I'll give Pete Fogg a shout as I go past – he can tow you out with his tractor."

"Thanks, Sam. Cheerio!"

Pat sat on the wall, to wait for Peter Fogg to come. Up on the hillside, he could see Alf and Dorothy Thompson busy with their hay-making. He could see the sheep and their lambs running and skipping in the green fields by the river.

Peter came at last. Pat was glad to see him.

"Hello, Peter," he said, "can you tow me out, please? My van's stuck in the mud."

"Easy," said Peter. "Sam told me you needed help. I'll just back up."

Peter turned his tractor in a gateway, then backed up until it was in front of Pat's van. Then he got his tow-rope out.

"Now then – just tie it on there," said Peter.

"Right-o," said Pat, tying it to a special bracket under the front bumper. Peter climbed on to the tractor again, and started the engine.

"Right?" he called.

"Yes, all ready," said Pat.

Peter drove slowly forward, until the rope was tight. He put more and more power on, until Pat's van began to ease out of the mud.

Soon it was on the hard road again. Peter took the rope off. Pat started his engine and waved to Peter.

"Bye! Thanks a lot!"

"Cheerio, Pat!"

Pat was on his way again.

When he arrived at the post-office, Mrs. Goggins said, "Morning, Pat. You're a bit late to-day."

So he told her all about how he had been stuck in the mud, and had to wait for Peter Fogg to come and pull him out. She showed him the Pencaster Gazette.

"Look," she said, "there's a picture of Major Forbes' bull. It's won first prize in the county show. Isn't it a magnificent beast? Have you seen it?"

"No," said Pat, "and I don't think I want to either."

"There's a letter for the major, so you might meet the bull: better keep a sharp look out."

"I'd run a mile if I saw it," said Pat. "Cheerio!"

Pat hadn't gone far, when he saw Ted Glen waving to him to stop.

"Some fool's left a gate open," he said, when Pat stopped. "I'll bet it's those campers. The sheep have got into the clover-field. It'll kill them if they eat too much. Can you give me a hand to drive them out?"

"Yes, of course I will," said Pat. "I used to work on a farm when I was a lad. Have they gone far, then?"

"You can see them up there. They have spread out a bit. "We'd better get after them."

The sheep were spread across the hillside, busily munching the clover that was so bad for them.

"You go that way, I'll go this," said Ted.

"Right!" said Pat.

What a time they had, catching those naughty sheep! The sheep ran all over the place. They jumped over walls and gates, dodged round trees and bushes, and hid in the long grass.

By the time Pat and Ted had chased them back into their own field, and closed the gate, they were hot and out of breath.

"Phew, that was warm work," said Ted.
"What's that funny noise?" said Pat.
"Hey up, it's that bull!" shouted Ted. "Run!"

They ran all down the steep hill, and jumped over the wall at the bottom. Ted said, "Ouch!" as he landed with a thump on the grass at the side of the road.

"What's up, Ted?" said Pat.

Ted could not stand up, and his leg seemed to be twisted.

"It's my ankle," said Ted. "By gum, it does hurt! Ouch, I can't get up. I think it's broken."

"Now what are we going to do?" said Pat. "You can't sit here till it gets better. I'd better go and get Dr. Gilbertson from the village. Won't be long!"

Pat drove away in his van, to Dr. Gilbertson's house. He gave the doctor her letters, then he told her about Ted's broken ankle.

"Oh dear, my car's in Pencaster being serviced," said Dr. Gilbertson.

"Then I'll take you in my van," said Pat.

So Dr. Gilbertson brought her bag and rode in the van. She sat in Jess's place, with Jess on her knee.

Ted was so glad to see the doctor. She soon bandaged his ankle up, with quite a bit of oooh-ing and ow-ing from Ted. It wasn't broken, just badly sprained.

"Try not to put too much weight on it, now," said the doctor.

Pat's walking-stick came in handy to help Ted to hobble to the van.

"Thanks, Pat," said Ted.

"You'll have to ride amongst the letters," said Pat.

"Easy, now."

Ted climbed in the back.

Jess rode back again on Dr. Gilbertson's knee.

    They took the doctor home. Then they took Ted home.

    Ted was glad to get home.

    "You all right, now?" said Pat.

    "I'll manage," said Ted. "Thanks for helping."

    "Cheerio!"

    "Bye!"

Pat was on his way again. He still had a lot of letters and parcels to deliver. He met Alf and Dorothy along the road, on their tractor.

"Hello, Alf!" called Pat.

"Hello, Pat," said Alf. "Thanks for getting the sheep back. It's the same thing every year – gates left open all over – we'll have to have words with them campers, won't we, Dot?"

Pat went on his way.

"What a morning, Jess! Rounding sheep up, dodging a bull, fetching the doctor – and now we're late with all this post. We'll have to get a move on, this afternoon."